Coast Guard Boats

Joanne Randolph

PowerKiDS press.

New York

For Riley, Deming, and Hannah

Published in 2008 by The Rosen Publishing Group, Inc.
29 East 21st Street, New York, NY 10010

First Edition

Book Design: Greg Tucker
Photo Researcher: Nicole Pristash

Photo Credits: Cover, pp. 5, 7, 9, 11, 13 Shutterstock.com; p. 15 © MENAHEM KAHANA/AFP/Getty Images; pp. 17, 23 by Chris Hondros/Getty Images; p. 19 by Tom Sperduto/U.S. Coast Guard via Getty Images; p. 21 by Phil Mislinki/Getty Images.

Library of Congress Cataloging-in-Publication Data

Randolph, Joanne.
  Coast Guard boats / Joanne Randolph. — 1st ed.
      p. cm. — (To the rescue!)
  Includes index.
  ISBN 978-1-4042-4152-7 (library binding)
  1. United States. Coast Guard—Boats—Juvenile literature. I. Title.
  VM397.R36 2008
  623.82'8—dc22
                                              2007021212

Manufactured in the United States of America

Contents

On the Lookout   4

A Helping Hand   10

Keeping Us Safe   12

Always Ready   16

Words to Know   24

Index   24

Web Sites   24

Coast Guard boats are on the lookout. They make sure we stay safe on the water.

U.S. COAST GUARD

25420

Coast Guard boats move quickly on the ocean waters.

There are many kinds of Coast Guard boats. Large boats, like this one, are called **cutters**.

1343   U. S. COAST GUARD

Coast Guard boats work to keep other boats and people safe during **storms**.

A ring like this one can be used to save someone who is in trouble in the water.

Coast Guard boats can help save people who are trapped by **floods**.

People in the Coast Guard sometimes need to chase people who do bad things.

COAST GUARD

25

Coast Guard boats keep the waters around big cities safe. This boat is watching over New York City.

Driving a Coast Guard boat is hard. Drivers use many tools to help them do their jobs.

Many people need help on the water every day. Coast Guard boats are always ready.

23

Words to Know

cutter

flood

storm

Index

P
people, 10, 14, 16

S
storms, 10

T
tools, 20

W
water(s), 4, 6, 12, 18, 22

Web Sites

Due to the changing nature of Internet links, PowerKids Press has developed an online list of Web sites related to the subject of this book. This site is updated regularly. Please use this link to access the list:
www.powerkidslinks.com/ttr/cboat/